Wild Cherry's Secret

Based on the Original Flower Fairies™ Books
by Cicely Mary Barker

Frederick Warne

High up above us, the
Flower Fairies of the trees
leap and swing.

These fairies dangle
daringly from their
branches, singing and
calling to one another.

All except one. Beautiful Wild Cherry
Blossom sits quietly, watching the others.

"Come and play
with us!" calls
cousin Cherry.
But Wild Cherry
shakes her head, and
clutches her branch.

Beech notices that
she looks a little scared.
"What's wrong?"
he calls out to her.
But Wild Cherry doesn't
answer.

That evening Wild Cherry
writes in her diary:

Dear Diary

All the other tree fairies
are such good climbers,
but I don't think
I'll ever be a real fairy acroba

The others are beginning to notice that I never join in. What should I do?

The next day, Mulberry is teasing Wild Cherry.

"What's the matter?" he asks. "Afraid of heights?"

"Don't worry,"
says Sweet Pea.
"I love you! And so do
the other babies. You
always watch over us".

Just as daylight begins to fade,
there is a cry from somewhere above
the fairies' heads. Without anybody
noticing, Baby Apple Blossom has
climbed far too high...

...She's stuck!

Everyone rushes to help.
"Just take my hand,"
says Lime Tree.

Crab-Apple holds out
her skirts and calls up
from below. "Jump!"

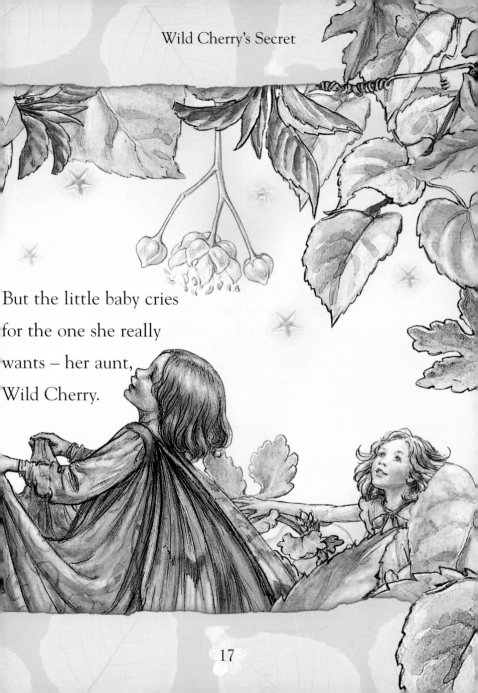

But the little baby cries
for the one she really
wants – her aunt,
Wild Cherry.

Quick as a flash, Wild
Cherry climbs to the rescue.
She scoops up the tearful
baby, and sets her safely on
a lower branch.

All the Flower Fairies are cheering, as Wild Cherry suddenly realizes what she has done. She beams proudly.

That night,
Wild Cherry writes
in her diary:

Dear Diary

I am proud that I

rescued baby Apple Blossom.

But that's all the leaping

about I want to do.

k I am the kind of
who likes to keep
 low branches and
's ok with me!
☆

FREDERICK WARNE

Published by the Penguin Group
Penguin Books Ltd, 80 Strand, London WC2R 0RL, England
New York, Australia, Canada, India, New Zealand, South Africa

This edition first published by Frederick Warne 2006
1 3 5 7 9 10 8 6 4 2

ISBN 0 7232 5357 9

Printed in China